KNEAD 'EM AND WEEP

RAISED AND GLAZED COZY MYSTERIES, BOOK 10

EMMA AINSLEY

SUMMER PRESCOTT BOOKS PUBLISHING

CHAPTER ONE

"I don't like the smell of fish or lakes or bait," Orson Hawley grumbled. He placed the last coffee syrup bottle in the wooden crate for the food truck.

"Which is why I'm not asking for you to go down there and run the food truck," Maggie Sharpe said. She hefted a tray of frozen cinnamon roll dough out the back door to the truck. Experience told her that packing frozen dough in the refrigerator was easier than making the rolls from scratch. The same was true for a variety of other treats. She had learned much from experience in the time she had owned Dogwood Donuts, including how to expand the business with a food truck.

"Who has a campout on a lake during a bass tournament anyway?" Orson continued.

"The campout is for the tournament, Orson," Ruby Cobb said. As Maggie's best friend and business partner, she had taken it upon herself to update the menu on the iPad for use in the food truck and Maggie didn't mind one bit.

"Thank goodness it's only a four-day weekend," Maggie muttered to Ruby. "He's likely to lose his mind if it goes on much longer than that."

"And he isn't even the one going to the lake." Ruby rolled her eyes but turned her head so only Maggie could see it.

"To be honest, I wonder if this is going to be an exercise in futility," Maggie said. "Who knows if bass tournament fishing campers are going to want coffee and donuts first thing in the morning?"

"We'll find out soon enough." Ruby smiled. "But I can't imagine anyone not wanting coffee and donuts."

As soon as the food truck was loaded for the following morning, Maggie whipped off her apron and threw it in the hamper inside the storeroom. "Are you ready?" she asked Ruby.

"Ready for what?"

"For dinner? The two of us at the Italian place? Did you forget?"

Ruby tossed a towel in her direction. "Of course

not," she said. "I've been looking forward to it all week."

"You aren't the only one," Maggie said. "Fact is, I've kept it a secret because I wanted tonight to be just you and me. Nothing against everybody else, I just want some best friend time."

"Gotcha," Ruby said with a wink. "It's been a while since we've had some time alone."

Maggie finished closing up the donut shop and hurried home for a fast shower before Ruby showed up at her house. The small house was quiet when she unlocked the door. Maggie felt a twinge of sadness at the silence. She missed the sound of her son Bradley knocking around the house and her tiny grandson Wyatt's coos and cries. On one hand, she was grateful for her son's ability to continue in the Navy after Wyatt's unexpected arrival, but on the other, she had grown used to a full house again.

She hurried to take a quick shower and dressed in a simple short-sleeve sweater and jeans. She dried her hair, brushed it out, and pulled it in a low ponytail. "Holy crap," she said and paused in the mirror. A single strand of gray hair over her right ear had multiplied overnight. "It's a whole patch of gray now."

Ruby arrived a mere twenty minutes after Maggie stepped out of the shower. "What's eating you?" she asked when Maggie opened the door. Without a word, Maggie pointed at the gray hairs above her ear.

"Oh, is that all?"

"Is that all? Last night it was a single hair," Maggie gasped. "How is this possible?"

"I'm going to pretend that you aren't asking me about gray hairs simply because I've got nearly a decade on you." She chuckled. "To answer your question, I don't know. I haven't had too many pop up myself.

My hair simply lightened after forty."

"Isn't that nice for you?" she joked. "Let's get to the restaurant. I know there's a bottle of red wine with our name on it.

Not long after, the two women were seated at a corner table at Curly's, their favorite Italian Restaurant. The place was quieter than they'd expected, but neither complained when they were able to get their wine and food quickly.

"The house is so quiet now," Maggie said over dinner. "I'm sad and glad at the same time."

"Have you heard from Bradley lately?"

Maggie twirled pasta around her fork and nodded her head. "He's in base housing and calls about every other day," she said. "We video call a lot, too. It's only been a few weeks, but I swear Wyatt has gained five pounds."

"So cute." Ruby shook her head. "Sometimes he makes me sad that I never had kids."

"I should send the pictures Bradley sends me to you," Maggie said.

"Oh, I get photos," Ruby said. She pulled her phone out to prove it. "Bradley has video-called me twice since he left. And he still calls me 'Aunt Ruby.'"

"Sounds like you've inherited the title whether you want it or not."

"Oh, I want the title." Ruby beamed. "It's nice, you know. I've already been shopping for Christmas presents."

"Oh, no," Maggie said. "Not you, too!"

"I can't help it. I don't think I've ever had a child to buy for. I've already picked out a couple of things for Wyatt and everyone else in my life and I don't see myself stopping any time soon."

"Well, I'd say I was feeling like I'm falling behind, but since it's only spring, I think I'll be okay."

"I know, I know." Ruby shook her head as she finished her meal. "Do you want any dessert?"

"I absolutely do, but how about we order it to take home? We can hang out at my house for a little while and talk and maybe even video chat Bradley and Wyatt. What do you think?"

"I think you read my mind. I knew I made you my best friend for a reason."

CHAPTER TWO

Maggie awakened early the next morning. She dressed quickly in yoga pants and a shirt with the donut shop's logo embroidered on the chest. It was a departure from the usual chef's style shirt she wore at the donut shop itself, but an extended length of time in the food truck called for comfort and the ability to dress up or down depending on the temperature.

She skipped a stop by the donut shop and drove straight to Dogwood Mountain Lake. She parked her car as close as she could get to the food truck. With Ruby's help, Maggie had managed to get the food truck parked in a spot meant for recreational vehicles, and as close to the lake as possible. The spot was perfect for foot traffic and within walking distance to three large picnic areas.

The air was chilly when she stepped out of her car. She slipped her large sweatshirt over her head, hoisted her tote bag over her shoulder, and headed down the path toward the food truck.

"It's the lake," a voice called to her. Maggie strained to see who was speaking to her in the early dawn light.

"Excuse me?" she asked.

"The air, the damp coolness," the voice drew closer. "I saw you when you stepped out of your car."

"Right," Maggie said a bit timidly. She wasn't too sure that she wanted to have a conversation with a stranger so early in the morning. "I'm just not used to it."

"Is this your rig?" the man asked. He moved closer to the food truck.

"It's a food truck, donuts, pastries, and coffee," Maggie said. "We're down here for the bass tournament." She studied the man a bit more closely under the light by her truck. He was tall, broad-chested, and gray. Age lined his face. His hair, and there was enough of it, stood up in thick, white shocks. He had the look of a wizened old cowboy. He was a handsome man, or he might have been. Maggie found herself mesmerized by his appearance.

"Ah, yes, the tournament," he said. "I heard there

was some sort of sport fishing game taking place down here over the next several days."

"This is the first year I've had the food truck," Maggie said, though she wasn't sure why she said anything at all. "I wanted to see if this might be something profitable for us."

"A noble effort at least." The man smiled. "How soon will you have the coffee ready?"

Maggie smiled back and shoved her key in the door. "Coffee will be ready as soon as I can get it started."

"Wonderful," he said. "You get that started and I will secure two seats for us in front of the lake."

Maggie set her bag down on the small table inside the food truck and pushed the 'on' button for the coffee pot. She removed the prepared cinnamon roll dough from the refrigerator and set it out on the counter to rise. Within moments, the coffee steamed in the pot, and the donut machine and deep fryer were on and heating up.

"I wasn't sure how you take it," she said when she walked down to the water's edge. The man was seated on one side of a park bench staring out across the water. The way he took his coffee wasn't the only thing she wasn't sure of, but something about the man drew her in. She felt compelled to talk to him.

"I take it however you make it, my dear." He sipped the coffee and closed his eyes to savor the flavor. "This is perfection."

Maggie glanced back at the food truck and sighed. She had a mountain of work to do before she opened up for the morning. But she decided a few moments on a park bench peering out over the lake wouldn't harm anyone.

"Are you from Dogwood Mountain?" Maggie asked.

"I am not," the man replied. "I'm staying at your delightful bed and breakfast up on the hill overlooking the town. If you have not had cause to visit that splendid old house, I would highly recommend it."

Maggie nodded. "I grew up visiting that house, long before it was the Dogwood House. My aunt owned it and I spent many hours curled up on the front porch with my head bent over a mystery novel. I'm Maggie Sharpe, by the way."

"Edmund Windsor," the man replied. He leaned toward her and extended his hand. "I should have known you had a literary soul. The way you gazed at that lake when you walked down the path told me everything I needed to know."

"You could tell that by the way I walked down the

path?" Maggie asked. She sipped her coffee again, intrigued but not frightened by the strange man seated next to her.

"I'm a bit of a literary soul myself," Edmund said. "That's why I'm here, a writer on a journey, or something like that." He chuckled and shook his head. Maggie thought at that exact moment he looked like every English professor in every novel she had ever read about English professors masquerading as brilliant novelists.

"Do you go on walks often?" Maggie asked.

"Why? Are you offering yourself as a companion during my stay here in this charming town?"

Maggie smiled. "Unfortunately, duty calls," she said and nodded toward the food truck. "I will be here all week, though. Are you a fan of donuts, Mr. Windsor?"

"Call me Edmund, and yes, donuts have their charms," he said.

"Well, hold on right here and I will return in a flash with breakfast," Maggie said. "I can't walk with you, but I'm more than happy to share breakfast with you."

"My dear, you have just made an old man very happy," Edmund said. Maggie watched as he settled

CHAPTER THREE

"Do you know who else is here in town?" one of the campers gathered outside of the order window asked. The air had lost the cool dampness of the early morning. Maggie turned on the fan in the truck and sent Ruby a text to send Orson along with another one when he had time.

"Who else is here in town? The Snap-on Tool Girls?" Maggie asked wryly. The crowd of hungry anglers hadn't thinned for longer than twenty minutes at a time since she opened. Nor had many of them showered, she observed.

"What the heck is a Snap-on Tool girl?" the man asked. He wore a thick beard and cargo shorts with leather sandals. Maggie guessed him to be in his early thirties.

"Tool calendars are a thing of the past," another customer called out behind him. "He wouldn't know what you're talking about."

Maggie chuckled uncomfortably and handed the first man his coffee. "Who else is around here, then?" she asked more sincerely.

"Edmund Windsor." The younger man smiled proudly as if he was the reason.

"She won't know who you're talking about, Jeffrey," the younger woman standing next to him said. "Any more than you'd know what a tool calendar girl is, of course."

"Actually, I do know who he is." Maggie handed out the last part of his order and smiled. Since her encounter with the novelist that morning, she had taken the time to read more about his literary works in the spare moments when the food truck wasn't busy. She wanted something to talk to him about when he made his way back early the next morning.

"So, you understand how ridiculously cool it is for him to be here in this little hick town at the same time we are here for the fishing tournament?" Jeffrey gushed.

"Funny, I wouldn't have expected an angler to be such a fanboy for a writer," an older woman said in the crowd behind him.

"Oh, Jeffrey really isn't much of a fisherman. He's only here because my father is a huge bass fishing enthusiast and he's trying to impress him," the girl next to him said.

"Gee, thanks for telling everyone and their brother, Emily," Jeffrey snapped.

"It's alright, son," said the older man right behind him. "I'm a bit of an Edmund Windsor fan myself. And I won this tournament about five years ago. I also know a lot about computers and trivia. I like photography, and I know what a tool girl is. I guess you could say I'm a pretty well rounded individual and I'd like to think all us fishermen are."

"Here you are," Maggie said, enjoying the fact that her customers were chatting. She handed the older man his coffee.

"My name is Elias Cavanaugh," he said to Jeffrey "If you get bored later on, come and find me down by the rest of the RVs. I'm in a dark brown fifth wheel. I'd love to talk books with you."

"Jeffrey Adams, and you're on." He shook Elias's hand before he turned back to Maggie. "If you run into Mr. Windsor again, please let him know that a few of us around here would love to meet him."

Maggie nodded but promised nothing. She handed

the bag of cinnamon rolls Elias had ordered out to him and began taking the next two orders.

An hour later, Orson pulled open the back door of the food truck and pushed the fan inside. "Here's your special delivery," he said and plopped down in the chair. "How about an iced coffee for an old man?"

"Coming right up." Maggie checked the window to make sure there were no customers and positioned the fan to blow across the truck before she pulled the iced coffee concentrate from the refrigerator. "Any particular flavor?"

"You know, I'm feeling like caramel pecan today," Orson said.

Maggie pulled two bottles of syrup from the storage cabinet and set them next to the tumbler. "And I suppose you have a perfect combination of caramel and pecan to educate me about." Maggie smirked. As her most particular employee, Orson always had something in mind.

Orson folded his arms over his chest and smiled like the Cheshire Cat. "Four shots caramel, three shots pecan," he said.

"Whoa, that's some seriously sweet iced coffee," she said and poured in the milk.

"And you're sweet to make it the way I like it," Orson said. Maggie stopped mixing in the milk and watched his face. "What? Why are you looking at me like that?"

"Because I figured there would be a snarky reply on the other side of it," Maggie said, checking the window again. "Are you feeling okay, Orson?"

"Yes, I'm feeling fine." He was a little agitated, but still not his normal sour self. "I just had a good morning is all."

"At the donut shop? Did someone come in and surprise you with a check for a million bucks or something?"

"Actually, no." Orson rolled his eyes. "I was just at the Dogwood House delivering morning coffee and breakfast."

Maggie set the iced coffee in front of him and smiled. "Oh, that explains it," she said.

"What explains what?" Orson asked. He sipped the coffee and smiled. "You're getting better at this."

"Thanks, I think," Maggie said. "So, how was Miss Gretchen today?" Gretchen LeClair was the owner of the Dogwood House Bed and Breakfast; the house Maggie's late Aunt Marjorie had owned before her death. Once in a while, it was clear that Gretchen was the object of Orson's fascination. The rest of the time, he never said a word about her or their relationship, whatever it was that it entailed.

"She's just fine, just fine." Orson smiled brightly. He caught himself and frowned immediately. "I mean, she was the same as normal, just like the old man who works for her. Why are you asking me so many questions?"

"Just making conversation." Maggie laughed. "Thanks for bringing the fan by. It gets a little humid down here."

"Watch out tomorrow," he said. "I think the weather is supposed to turn a bit cooler."

Orson left a few minutes later and Maggie returned to the window. Things were quiet for a while longer and she used the time to clean up anything she'd missed before. She liked to clean as she went rather than try to work in a mess. Eventually, customers started arriving again and came in a steady stream for the next couple of hours. At last, she finally had a lull in business, and Ruby appeared around then with boxed lunches.

"I don't recall ever seeing this many people at the lake," Ruby said when she set the final crate of lunches in the refrigerator. "This is insane."

Maggie took her own lunch from the stack and sat at the table. "I heard someone say this morning that the campground is full to capacity. This is the biggest turnout for the bass tournament ever."

"Gretchen told Orson that the bed and breakfast is full as well."

"I met one of her guests this morning," Maggie said as she started eating. "His name is Edmund Windsor."

Ruby's eyes widened. "The author? That's incredible!"

"So, you know who he is, then?" Maggie asked. "By the way, this apple slaw is the best ever."

"Thanks, and I am shocked that you haven't heard of him before," Ruby said. "You're a voracious reader."

"I'm just not that familiar with his particular genre," Maggie said. "He writes fantasy. I read mystery and suspense."

"He has a very loyal following. I don't think he's the most widely known writer, but his fans are pretty serious about their devotion to him," Ruby explained.

"It was strange," Maggie said. "I met two or three campers this morning who knew who he was."

"Among the bass tournament people?"

Maggie nodded her reply as she was too busy enjoying Ruby's food to talk.

"Well, I've been wrong before. Perhaps Edmund Windsor has an audience within the bass fisherman groups. Stranger things have happened."

CHAPTER FOUR

Maggie headed out fifteen minutes earlier than she had the morning before. She wanted to start the donuts before her writer friend made his way down the lakeshore to where she was parked. While the coffee brewed, Maggie set two cinnamon rolls she had brought from home in the oven to bake. She warmed a small portion of buttercream frosting, just to make the cinnamon rolls richer.

For herself, Maggie began to mix a cinnamon latte after the coffee was brewed. Whether Edmund would like something more exotic than the morning before, she wasn't sure. She peered out the windows for a sign of him. Seeing nothing, she turned back to the coffee.

"I guess I'll make him a latte, too," she said. The

worst thing that could happen was a request for black coffee, instead. A couple of minutes later, Maggie stepped out of the back of the food truck. She carried both lattes in paper cups.

"There you are, my dear," Edmund called out to her in the distance. Maggie raised one of the coffee cups in his direction. She gazed over the campsites while Edmund made his way closer to her. Fortunately, few lights burned in the early morning darkness. She was grateful that none of the writer's fans appeared to be aware of his presence on the lakeshore.

"I hope you're in the mood for something a little different this morning." Maggie handed the cup to him and waited while he took his first sip.

"Oh, my darling friend. You have outdone yourself. I am a true fan of cinnamon."

"That's a good thing," Maggie said. "Because our cinnamon rolls will be ready in a moment. And I have plans to send two dozen mini donuts rolled in cinnamon and sugar with you."

Edmund placed his hand dramatically on his chest. "You know the way to an old man's heart. Shall we retire to the shore?" he asked.

"I'll be right back with breakfast," she said and handed her cup to him.

A moment later, they walked down to the park bench on the shore and sat down. Maggie passed a paper food tray over to him and took her coffee back. They watched as the buoys bobbed up and down on the waves, illuminated by lights across the lake. "Beautiful morning," Edmund said at last. "I always find myself drawn to the water. Whether it's on the seashore or a lakeshore, my soul draws me in."

"Did you grow up on the water?" Maggie asked. She found herself staring out over the lake. Even in the low morning light, the gentle movement of the water mesmerized her. She forgot to rush or worry about anything.

"No. Unfortunately, I am unable to enjoy the water myself," Edmund said. "But water inspires me. I write about it in every world I create. It plays a significant role in every plot."

"You write fantasy, right?"

"High fantasy, if you want to split hairs about it." He turned to her. "You said you read mystery if I remember correctly. Take your favorite noir mystery novel and set it in an alternative world."

"So, Dick Tracy meets Star Wars?"

"Oh, no. Nothing like that. Not like that at all," he said. "My worlds are never alien worlds, so to speak. I don't write science fiction. I write entire worlds that might be an alternative to earth. Think of Lord of the Rings set on a distant world."

"And add a noir mystery," Maggie said as she worked on eating the warm cinnamon roll.

"Now you've got it." Edmund sipped his coffee and studied the waves for a moment. "I ventured toward horror, but only for a short time."

"Why only for a short time?" Maggie asked. "What happened?"

Edmund shrugged. "It wasn't authentic. Not for me, anyway," he said. "As a writer, or at least, for this writer, in order to create a world like that, I have to be able to close my eyes and immerse my mind in it. I just couldn't do that with horror. The only reason I started was because I was going through a difficult time in my life and I needed an outlet, but it is not for me. I'll leave it to the better, more talented folks."

"Did you ever publish any of them?"

"Oh, yes," he said. "Some of my biggest royalty checks came from those novels. I published five but planned twice that many."

"You just stopped writing them?" Maggie asked. She was enthralled by the discussion.

Edmund shook his head slowly. "Not abruptly, really. But I did finish the final novel in a way that left many readers rather angry at me. Sales of my other books suffered slightly, but it was short-lived," he said. He tipped his cup in her direction. "And it was worth every lost sale. Life is nothing if you cannot live it authentically."

Maggie speared the center of the cinnamon roll on her fork and plopped the final bite in her mouth. She was about to ask more questions when a large rain-drop landed on her forehead. "I think we're about to get soaked," she said and stood quickly. "Would you like to come inside the food truck and wait it out?"

Edmund stood and gripped Maggie by the arm. "I'm afraid I am at your mercy, my dear," he said. "Lead the way."

They reached the food truck a split second before the heavens opened up and the downpour pinged off of the roof. "Edmund," Maggie gasped when they were inside. "Your face! What's wrong?"

"It's the rain." He slumped down in the chair and sighed.

The angry red marks on his face disappeared almost as quickly as they'd come. Maggie kept her questions to herself. The last thing she wanted was to push the seemingly private man into revealing more about himself than he wanted. He liked to talk about his writing, but not himself and that was okay with her.

While she worked, Edmund sat at the small corner table and regaled her with stories about his travels and his life as an author. She breezed through the morning tasks while she listened. She smiled as he spoke and asked only a minimal amount of questions. By the time the sun peeked over the horizon, she felt as though she had been on a grand adventure.

"I should go," Edmund announced when Maggie turned the "Open" sign on. "I do not desire meeting fans out while I walk."

"I can understand that." Maggie packed his donuts in a sack and handed them over. "I met a few of them yesterday. Hard to believe bass fishermen have an eye for good literature."

"I am aware that there are fans among them if you want to call them that," he grumbled.

"Would you like a ride back to the Dogwood House? I can call one of my crew members to come and take over," Maggie offered.

"Not at all, my dear," Edmund replied, peering out the window to make sure the rain had stopped. "Am I to understand from your comments that you would be open to reading one of my novels?"

Maggie grinned. "I already ordered one online," she said.

"Oh, poo." Edmund frowned. "That won't do.

Tomorrow morning you shall have a signed copy of the first book in my latest series."

"Oh, you don't need to do that," Maggie assured him.

Edmund opened the door and stepped out of the food truck. He bowed dramatically. "It would be my pleasure, my lady," he said. "Until we meet again."

"See you in the morning, Edmund." Maggie chuckled.

CHAPTER FIVE

"Alright, you're two days in. How's it going at the lake?" Brett asked Maggie when they met up at the donut shop later that afternoon. Both had been so busy with their careers lately that for the last week, the majority of their time spent together was at the donut shop. It worked out for both of them, though, since Maggie owned the place and Brett couldn't seem to say no to her coffee and donuts. As the chief of police in Dogwood Mountain, none of his officers were upset about all the treats he brought them, either.

"Sales are out of sight if that's what you're asking," she said. "I closed up an hour early this afternoon because I ran out of boxed lunches."

He took a seat on a barstool at the counter across from where she stood. "I'm glad it's going so well for you. The police on the other hand, well, we've had to deal with a couple of skirmishes overnight among the campers. I can't wait for this bass tournament to be over."

"I'm surprised to hear you say that," Ruby said. She carried a tray of lunches and placed it in the stainless-steel refrigerator. "I thought everyone was excited about the tournament."

Brett shook his head. "You'd be surprised how rowdy those people can be."

Myra Sawyer came through the swinging door from the kitchen with another tray for Ruby. "I heard they were planning on another tournament next week." Maggie's young employee passed the tray over and shrugged. "Of course, I don't know a thing about fishing…"

Brett nodded. "That happens every year," he said. "A group of the most diehard fishermen stick around another few days to continue the tradition. But mostly they just hang out on the shore and drink beer."

"Hopefully the ones who stick around aren't the same ones causing trouble for you now," Maggie said to Brett. She always preferred when he had a light schedule so they could spend more time together and since that hadn't been happening lately, she'd been looking forward to things changing after the tournament was over.

"Oh, I meant to ask you, how was your friend this morning?" Ruby placed the empty tray on the counter and refilled her coffee cup. She turned to Maggie and waited eagerly for a reply.

"What friend?" Brett asked immediately. Maggie ignored the look on Myra's face when he asked. She thought his desire to be protective was sweet.

"A mysterious writer named Edmund." Myra grinned. Maggie shot her a sideways look. "What? From everything you said about him, he seems mysterious!"

"He's an older man who has taken a shine to our friend here," Ruby said. "He takes walks to the lake every morning from the Dogwood House where he's staying."

Maggie felt the need to explain further when she saw the look on Brett's face. "I ran into him yesterday morning, and now it's a habit to sit on a bench overlooking the lake." She looked over at Brett and continued, trying not to laugh at his pursed lips and clenched jaw. "Well, I guess I wouldn't say it's a habit. It's only happened twice so far."

"So far?" Brett asked slowly.

"I like talking with him and will probably do it

again. It's nice to chat with a writer like that." Maggie had always dreamed of being a writer herself, but it had never taken off. She loved how busy she was at the donut shop, but her love of the literary world hadn't just gone away. "He tries to avoid his fans, I think. That's why he walks so early in the morning."

"'Fans' is short for fanatics," Orson offered from his seat at the old timer's table. "I talked to him myself if you don't believe me. He's very private. And he's had many run-ins with crazy fans."

"Oh, wow," Maggie said. She had heard Edmund's descriptions about his fans, but not the ugly side of it all. "He's such a nice man. I could sit and listen to him talk about being a writer for hours."

"I didn't know you were that interested in writers," Brett said.

Maggie laughed. "I'm not interested in writers, exactly. You know I read a lot. I've always read a lot," she said. "I don't know if I'll ever get to write something myself or not but listening to what one has to say is pretty cool in my book."

Orson and Ruby cracked up at her clever play on words.

Brett laughed then. "You always had your face shoved in a book in high school," he said. "I used to wonder what was so interesting that you didn't see the people around you, watching you all the time." As soon as he spoke, the room was silent. Brett looked around for a moment, and then seemed to realize what he had said. "Not to say that I was watching you. No, that's not what I meant at all."

"So, there were other people watching me?" Maggie grinned. "That's not creepy in the least."

"Don't worry about it, Chief." Orson reached over and slapped him on the back. "I think it's pretty obvious that you've had a thing for Maggie since, well forever. No big deal that you needed to go through three wives to finally realize it."

"Remind me, Orson," Brett said, not even bothering to look at him. "How are you and Gretchen doing?"

"Point taken." Orson grumbled and all the men at his table chuckled and murmured. He didn't talk about his own relationship yet seemed rather pushy when it came to everyone else.

"I should get going," Brett announced.

"You aren't mad, are you?" Maggie asked, worried that Orson had said too much. He was a grown man, but she felt responsible for him and his outbursts.

"Not in the least. He's right, but I can't let him know that," Brett whispered.

"Looks like you finally caught on." Ruby laughed. "He means no harm."

Brett nodded. "I'll see you all later," he said and went for the door.

Maggie followed Ruby to the kitchen. "Why don't I come by a little earlier with reinforcements tomorrow? Maybe we'll stay ahead of the lunch crowd a little better that way. That and I wouldn't hate to meet Edmund myself."

"Sounds like a plan," Maggie agreed. "I thought I'd hang around here after we close up for the day and do a little more prep work for tomorrow morning, anyway."

"I'll stick around and help you. We'll get everything restocked and prepped for tomorrow and then we can hang out at my house for a little while if you want. Does that sound like a good idea?"

"It does indeed." She wanted to make it an early night, but an evening around a bonfire sounded like a good way to relax. "Is anyone else stopping by?"

"Oh, the usual suspects," Ruby said with a wink. The "usual suspects" meant Orson, Myra, Brett, and the young police officer, Brooks Macklin, who had become an important part of their small group of friends. Myra was especially fond of his company.

"Why do I feel like you have something up your sleeve?" Maggie asked, eyeing her friend.

"Oh, no reason." Ruby smiled. "Except that, I might have invited another Dogwood Mountain resident."

"Like who?"

"I thought it would be nice to invite Gretchen," Ruby said. "She almost never comes to anything we do, and I feel like she definitely has a place with us."

"You're either crazy or looking to cause trouble!" Maggie clapped her hands together and smiled. "Don't you think Orson will have your head for this?"

"Think of it this way," Ruby said. "With as little as Orson says about him and Gretchen, as far as I'm concerned they aren't even a couple. Gretchen is our friend and I thought it would be nice to include her. The rest, well, I guess we'll cross that bridge when we come to it."

"You're throwing around the word we an awful lot. I'm not sure I want to be part of your shenanigans," Maggie teased.

Ruby responded by tossing her apron at Maggie. "We'll finish up here and I'll run by the grocery store on my way home. If you don't hear from me, it's because Orson found out early that I invited Gretchen. That'd be one easy murder to solve."

"Let's hope it isn't that drastic." Maggie laughed.

"I think I'll take a few more things by the food truck before I head home to clean up, then I'll make my way over to your place."

"You're going back to the lake?"

"Yeah," Maggie said. "Might as well make life even simpler tomorrow morning. Having you there will be helpful, but with as busy as it's been there, we can use all the extra prep work possible." She walked to the cooler and began carefully placing the dough for the following morning into crates. She hefted the crate to her car and returned for the lunch boxes. Ruby followed with more crates.

"Are you sure you don't want help taking these to the food truck?" Ruby closed the trunk lid and waited. "I can follow you over there in the truck and help you put everything inside."

"That's okay," Maggie said. "I won't be there long. By the time you get back from the store, I'll probably already be on my way to your house."

"Alright," Ruby agreed "Just don't bring a mess of fish out there with you."

Maggie wrinkled her nose. "If I never smell another raw fish again, it will still be too soon."

CHAPTER SIX

As soon as she opened the food truck and began unloading the food from her car, a line formed outside of the serving window. "When will you be open again?" a voice called out. Maggie looked up from her trunk.

"Tomorrow morning at six."

"Seriously? You're not going to open up for us right now?" Jeffrey, the man who was a fan of Edmund Windsor, stared back at her.

"I'm not open right now. This is a breakfast and lunch operation."

"Do you have anything left over from this morning?" he asked.

Maggie felt herself growing more annoyed by the second. She wanted to accommodate her customers, but there was only so much she could do. "Sadly, we sold out of everything," she said, not actually sad, it was a good thing. "But there's a nice diner in downtown Dogwood Mountain that stays open until six. Oh, and the Italian place just outside of town is wonderful."

"Come on," Jeffrey persisted. "Just open back up for an hour or two."

"If you are that hungry for donuts, I expect to see you bright and early in the morning," Maggie said with a forced smile. She shut and locked the food truck door behind her. While she worked to arrange the lunches in the refrigerator, she tried to keep an eye on the crowd outside without appearing obvious. For reasons she could not understand, Jeffrey and his girlfriend, Emily, continued to talk loudly in front of the crowd about the closure of the food truck.

Thirty minutes later, the crowd was gone, and Maggie finished up her work and managed to leave without anyone else confronting her. She pulled out of the maze of roads surrounding the lake and headed for home. As she drove, she heard the wail of a siren in the distance.

"Sounds like the campers might be getting an early start on the party tonight," she said to herself.

After a quick shower, Maggie headed back out of

town toward Ruby's farm. She arrived a little later than she had planned. Myra, Brooks, Orson, and Gretchen were already seated around the bonfire.

"You okay?" Myra asked her as soon as she stepped out of her car. "We were starting to get worried."

Maggie glanced at the clock on her phone. "I'm less than a half-hour later than I said I would be," she said. "Why were you worried?"

Ruby emerged from the back door with two glasses of red wine. She handed one directly to Maggie. "Have you talked to Brett?"

Maggie took the glass and eyed her best friend carefully. "Did something happen to Brett?" she asked. "He runs late sometimes, but I'm sure he'll be here soon. Why is everyone acting so weird?"

"Have a seat, Maggie," Ruby said. She led her to her favorite Adirondack chair.

"Seriously," Maggie snapped. "Did something happen to Brett? Is he alright? Brooks?"

"Brett is fine," Brooks answered. He leaned forward and reached for her hand. "He's on duty. We're all acting weird because we wondered if you had heard about Edmund Windsor."

"What about him?"

Brooks tightened his grip on her hand. "He was

just found dead along the shores of Dogwood Mountain Lake."

"Oh, no," Maggie said. Tears immediately sprang to her eyes. "He's dead?"

Brooks nodded his head slowly. "I know you were getting close to him. I'm sorry to have to tell you."

"Wait a minute," Maggie said. "How was he found? I mean, was he hurt?"

"Apparently he was walking along the shore when he passed away," Brooks said.

"That doesn't sound right," Maggie said. "Edmund didn't like to walk in the middle of the day."

Brooks released her hand and shrugged. "Maybe he decided it was a nice day and decided to see the lake in the daytime."

"She's right," Gretchen spoke up. "He was very adamant about that. In fact, he asked for peace and quiet from late mornings until the middle of the afternoon so he could write and sleep as desired."

"That doesn't necessarily mean anything," Brooks said. "You know there will be an investigation."

"It strikes me as odd," Gretchen continued. "When I left the house to come here for the evening, I swore Mr. Windsor was still in his room. I'm pretty sure I could hear the typewriter."

"Typewriter? Who still uses a typewriter?" Orson asked.

"Edmund Windsor insisted on it," Myra said. "I looked him up after Maggie met him. The man certainly had a lot of quirks. He isn't much for technology at all."

"It's true. Edmund didn't care for computers. I read an interview about how he relies on a personal secretary to take his typewritten manuscripts and transcribe them onto a computer for him," Maggie said.

"Okay, look," Brooks said. "I'm not sure that this proves anything, but I'll let Brett know."

"I just can't believe he's dead," Maggie said. She buried her head in her hands. "I was just at the lake. What if I could have prevented this?"

"You couldn't have. He was found on the opposite end from where the tournament is and where your truck is parked. There's no way you could have prevented anything unless you were walking around when you were there."

"I wasn't, it's just so hard to understand. He didn't deserve this."

"I had no idea you were so close to him," Brooks said differently than he had before. The tone of his voice had changed.

Maggie looked up and studied his face. She

wasn't sure what she was looking for, but what she found were hard curiosity and some concern. "Not a relationship, no," she said. "I only just met him. We sat and had coffee and breakfast by the lake twice. It hadn't been long, but he was such a sweet man. I already told Brett all this."

His face softened. "He seemed like an interesting man, that's for sure," he said. "What I don't know is why anyone would want to murder him."

"Murder?" Maggie gasped. "You didn't make it sound like that when you said he passed away."

Brooks nodded his head slowly. "Edmund Windsor was strangled to death."

CHAPTER SEVEN

Maggie woke late the next morning. She panicked for a moment, and then remembered that her morning lake companion would not be meeting her before the food truck opened. She couldn't wrap her mind around the fact that he was dead, let alone murdered. Who on earth would kill an aged fantasy author? Edmund was a self-described introvert. He rarely interacted with people. She knew this, and she counted her few interactions with him precious because of it.

She moved through the motions of getting ready, driving to the lake, and setting up the food truck for a six o'clock opening. At ten minutes before six, Maggie poured herself a simple cup of black coffee. She stirred in a small amount of creamer and walked out of the back door and stood for a moment, watching the lake from afar. She glanced back over her shoulder at the food truck and then sighed. She had to take advantage of the fact that Edmund was found so far away from where the event was that the tournament was still on, but she needed one last look at the lake in his memory.

She had to do it. Let the donut shop wait on her for once. Walking toward the shore, Maggie sipped her coffee and thought of her friend. She reached the park bench and sat down. The water was still but soon the lake would be filled with boats and anglers dropping their lines in the water hoping to snag a championship catch and finish the tournament on top.

"At least this thing is almost over," a voice came out of nowhere. Maggie looked up. Jeffrey, her customer from the first morning, walked around the side of the bench and sat down next to her. "I'll be so glad when this is a memory."

Maggie moved toward the edge of the bench. "Can I help you with something?"

"Oh, no," Jeffrey said and waved her off. "Not right now, anyway. I'm sure I'll be back for something later. I just came down here because I couldn't sleep."

"Are you normally asleep at six in the morning?" Maggie asked.

Jeffrey shrugged. "Depends. I'm a nontraditional sleeper," he said. "Actually, is there any chance I could get a cup of coffee?"

Maggie stood up. She tried to decide at that moment what she wanted to do. On one hand, she resented the man for disturbing her reflection on Edmund's death, but on the other, the food truck was open, and it was time for her to get to work. She couldn't blame the man for wanting coffee.

"I'm heading to the truck now. You're welcome to come over to get yourself a cup when you're ready."

She stood and walked back up the path without looking back at him.

Maggie locked the truck door behind her and worked through the last-minute preparations for the morning. When the first batch of mini donuts was ready, she rolled them in cinnamon sugar and placed them in the warmer under the front counter. She turned on the neon open sign and unlocked the front windows at just two minutes after six. A line had already formed outside. She opened a window and scanned the crowd for signs of Jeffrey but didn't see him. Something about that guy gave her the creeps.

A few moments later, Maggie was busy handing

out lattes and cups of black coffee along with dozens of mini donut orders. She worked her way through the first long line and paused to add batter to the mini donut machine. A quick glance at the container under the counter told her that her time would have been better spent refilling the containers than sitting on a park bench watching the lake before dawn. She took another order and started a latte, then grabbed the container and headed to the small cooler at the back of the truck.

She opened the cooler door and heard a noise just outside. At first, she figured a squirrel, or another pest was messing around. A second later, she changed her mind when she heard the sound of a man clearing his throat. Maggie glanced out the front first, then turned back. She unlocked the door and flung it wide open. Jeffrey stood just outside the food truck. He looked up at her, his eyes wide.

"What in the heck are you doing back here?" Maggie demanded. "You have no business nosing around the back of my food truck! What are you looking for?"

He stared at her for a moment, and then his face hardened. "I was waiting for that cup of coffee you promised me over an hour ago."

Maggie's hands went to her hips. "I never

promised you a thing." she said. "There are two windows on the front of this truck. One is for ordering and the other is the one I use to hand you the coffee or donuts or whatever, after you have paid for it."

"What? No coffee on the house? Why not? You were more than happy to give that old man free coffee and donuts! Why not me?" Jeffrey spat his words back at her.

"I'm not sure who you are referring to." Maggie glared at him. "But you're more than welcome to head to the front and place an order if you can manage to rein in your negativity."

"You know good and well I'm talking about Edmund Windsor. I don't see the difference between him and me, aside from the fact that he's a loser and I'm not. Which is even more reason for you to serve me free stuff."

"Get out of here!" Maggie shouted. She could hear the collective reaction from the small line in the front of her food truck. "I am not going to serve you anything!"

"Hey, hey," Brett's voice called out from the side of the truck. She heard him before she saw him. He came into view and stood behind Jeffrey. "Is there a problem here?"

Maggie fought the urge to demure her reaction.

"Yes, actually, there is a problem," she said. "This man was messing around back here. I could hear him through the doors. And when I opened the doors, he said that I had promised him free coffee, which I did not!"

"Okay, buddy," Brett said firmly. "You need to get out of here. Stay away from the food truck."

"No," Jeffrey said flatly. "I will not leave. And I will be served my free coffee. For that matter, she needs to throw in a bag of free donuts for all this undue stress she's causing me."

"'She' will not be giving you a thing for free," Maggie said. "You should listen to the police chief and get out of here."

Jeffrey shook his head. "Not happening. I know my rights. This is public land," he said. "I demand my rights."

"I don't know where you're from, but you are not entitled to anything free," Brett said. "And this is not public land. This space has been rented by the donut shop. It's the same as a lease on a house. You are not entitled to step foot near this space unless you plan on ordering something and paying for it, which unfortunately for you, is no longer an option."

"You're wrong," Jeffrey said. "I can and I will wait right here and demand my food." He placed one foot up on the back bumper of the truck and folded his arms over his chest. He stared at Brett for a long moment.

"I have to go wait on my other customers," Maggie said. She looked at Brett. "Please don't leave him back here." Brett nodded at her before she shut and locked the door again. Maggie returned to the window and apologized profusely to the waiting crowd. She began filling three orders right away, trying to shake away her annoyance.

CHAPTER EIGHT

"I want my coffee," Jeffrey yelled from the back of the truck not two minutes later. She felt the truck begin to shake. "Do you hear me, lady? Give me my stuff!"

"Alright, that's enough," Brett yelled. The shaking stopped and Maggie could hear the sounds of a scuffle.

She turned back to the older man standing outside her window and smiled. "I'm so sorry about that," she said and handed over his coffee.

"I'm not," the man said. "That guy is a menace. He's always invading campsites and making a nuisance of himself."

"Really?"

"Yeah," the man said. Several others nodded their

heads in agreement. "He's not even fishing in the tournament. I have no idea why he is even here."

"I thought he was here with a woman," Maggie said. She handed over the man's sack of donuts.

"I think she went somewhere else," another man in the crowd added. "Probably sick of his crap."

"But he has a campsite," the first man said. "At least, I can see his tent from my campsite. I have a pop-up parked right down there by the dock."

"Okay." Maggie filed the tidbit of information in her mind and went back to serving her customers. She looked up only once when Brett walked by leading a handcuffed Jeffrey away from the food truck. Applause erupted from the small crowd. Maggie bit her lip to prevent the smile that threatened to overtake her face.

"I take it you aren't sad to see him go." Elias Cavanaugh stood outside her window. Maggie recognized him from the first day of the tournament, the same time she had met Jeffrey and it seemed the two men had it hit off. "I'll take one of those cinnamon lattes and a vanilla bean scone."

"Coming right up," she said. She noted the bucket hat on his head covered with several fishing lures. "I'm surprised that you aren't out on the boat like the rest of them."

Elias shrugged. "I'm older than most of these guys. I go out a little later so my blood pressure medicine can work through my system first if you know what I mean. It just makes the day easier when I don't have to keep running up to the docks."

Maggie figured he was referring to the outdoor portable restrooms that lined one of the docks across the lake. "I can understand that."

"Besides, it's fun to start a little later and have my fresh donuts with me to enjoy a little longer." He smiled. "You sure have a good thing going here. I wish you had a store down south where I'm from."

"Oh yeah? And where are you from?"

"Pawhuska, northwest of Tulsa." He smiled. "Any thoughts of expansion down Oklahoma way?"

Maggie shook her head. "I can't imagine expanding in this state, let alone another one. Although, my son is stationed down by Lawton. He just moved down there with my grandson. Oklahoma might be tempting."

"Well, if you ever decide to pull up stakes and head down that way, you let me know." Elias raised his coffee cup to her and headed back toward the lake.

Maggie waited on the next customer in line. When she had a little break, she fixed a cup of iced coffee and settled in on one of the chairs. She checked her phone for word from Brett. No messages appeared. She was curious about the fate of the man who had harassed her, so curious that she decided to look him up online.

She typed "Jeffrey Adams" into a search engine and waited for his profile to pop up. In a matter of seconds, she found him. His background picture was the very lake she was parked at. She scrolled down at his public information and found a photo of the pretty young woman standing next to him on the main dock.

She recognized the young woman as Emily, the daughter of the bass fisherman Jeffrey was trying to impress. If he acted in any way around her family like he had that morning, Maggie wondered why they bothered dating at all. She clicked on the name Emily Henson, tagged in the photo. Emily's profile page popped up. Right away Maggie noted the sad face emojis and the relationship status update.

"Single," it said, followed by tons of crying faces in the comments. Maggie looked around for a few more minutes. It was clear they had just broken off their relationship. She clicked back to Jeffrey's profile. There was no mention of a breakup at all. In fact, the photo of the two of them together on the dock had been captioned "Love of my life" only a couple of hours before.

"That's interesting." She took a screenshot of his page and scrolled down a little further. The rest of the page was filled with various rants about everything under the sun.

Maggie looked up from her phone. Several more people were heading down the parking lot toward her food truck. She glanced down at the screen once more, ready to shut it off and prepare for another crowd and noticed a post under the last meme. She scrolled down to a photo of Edmund Windsor smiling beside a table filled with books. He was considerably younger and slimmer. His hand rested on a stack of books. Maggie pinched the screen to read the title. "Neighborhood Watchers," she said aloud.

She quickly googled the book title and Edmund Windsor's name. "It's a series," she read, and then noted the description.

Horror.

"That must be the series he stopped writing," she said. She scrolled further down Jeffrey's profile and held her breath. The next post was another picture of Edmund with the word "traitor" photoshopped over his face. The word was written in dark red block letters.

"Oh, no," she said. Reluctantly, she set her phone down and went back to work. She knew there was

CHAPTER NINE

Myra showed up at ten to help. Together they carried trays of boxed lunches in and set them up in the refrigerator. "I'm not complaining, but why are you here instead of Ruby? Did something happen?" Maggie asked as they worked.

"Jeez, you could give somebody a complex," Myra teased. "I asked Ruby if I could come because I want to talk to you about something."

"Uh oh. I don't know if I like the sound of that," Maggie said. She leaned against the counter to rest for a moment.

"It's nothing bad," Myra assured her. "Ruby said you were really busy yesterday, so I hope I brought enough."

"It looks like plenty." She pointed to the warmer.

"I over-prepared for the morning crowd, I think. I have two dozen sacks of mini donuts left."

"You should take those around and give them out for free," Myra suggested. "Maybe you can find out something about your writer friend's death."

Maggie dropped her hands to her side and stared at Myra for a moment. Myra shifted her weight from one foot to the other. "Did I say something wrong?" she asked.

"Oh, no!" Maggie shook her head and reached for Myra's hands. "I was just wondering if you had been a fly on the wall a little while ago! I was doing a little social media stalking for that very purpose."

"Great minds." Myra opened up the warmer and began pulling out the bags. "Let's get you fixed up then," she said. "I'll make you something for lunch so you can rest when you get back."

"Oh, I'll just eat a boxed lunch," Maggie said.

Myra shook her head. "Nope," she said. "I have plans. I want you to try something."

"Now, I'm intrigued," Maggie said.

"You should be. I'm preparing quite a treat for you. Now, go on out there and investigate to your little heart's content."

Maggie grabbed her phone from the table in the back and headed out the door with the extra donuts in a crate. She headed straight for the camping area Elias Cavanaugh had indicated. She walked down the blacktop road to the grassy area and down a decently long road that led away from the lake and to a camping area. A group of women was seated in camping chairs in a half-circle facing the lake.

"Hello," she said to the women. "I have some extra mini donuts here."

"We'll take them!" An older woman with spiky burgundy hair hopped up from her chair. Maggie was surprised at her agility, given her age. "What kind do you have?"

"Who cares, Angie," another woman said. "We aren't picky, especially when it's free donuts."

Maggie laughed and handed over three sacks. "I hope that's enough," she said.

"Oh, honey," Angie said as she reached into the first sack. "I thought you were just going to hand over one. We'll gladly take three."

Maggie smiled and headed further into the campground. She passed several tent sites. Most of them were empty for the time being. Given the number of boats on the lake, she wasn't surprised. She walked for a few moments and then spotted a woman standing among several small children close to a picnic table between two large tents. The closer she was, the more children she could see.

"Ma'am," she called out. "My name is Maggie Sharpe and I own that food truck over there." She pointed toward the RV spot.

"Oh, we love donuts," a little girl said. Maggie looked down at the small child. She guessed her to be about four. Her long, blonde hair was pulled back into two braids.

"Macy," the woman warned. "We do not beg."

"I'm sorry, Mama," the little girl said. Her face fell and she sat down at the picnic table.

"How can I help you?" the mother asked.

"Oh, I didn't mean to cause any problems," Maggie said. "I was actually walking around looking for someone who might like a sack of mini donuts. I made a few too many this morning."

"Oh, I'm sorry. We already have enough food around here." Maggie interpreted her comments to mean that she didn't have extra money for the treat.

"Well," Maggie said. "It would be a huge help to me if someone could enjoy these extra donuts. I can't sell them now. They have been in the warmer for too long. They are still fresh and warm, but I have a strict two-hour limit for the warmer."

"What's a warmer?" the little girl asked.

"It's a place where I put the donuts I make to keep them warm." Maggie turned back to the woman. "Is it okay to give them some?"

"Oh, yes," the woman said. She blushed slightly. "I didn't realize you were giving them away."

"How many kiddos do you have?" Maggie asked.

"There's ten of us," the little girl shouted. She jumped up from her seat and clapped her hands. As soon as she caught the look on her mother's face, she closed her mouth abruptly and sat back down.

"I'm sorry," the woman said quietly. "We are working on our manners this morning."

Maggie gazed around at the other children. Each one was dressed in clean, neat clothing. There was nothing out of place, and nothing that pointed to a family camping trip at the lake. "Well," she said and reached into the crate. "I think I have found a home for a few bags at least."

"My daddy and my brudders will be back in a little while," the little girl offered. "My gramma is over there." She stuck her thumb out behind her and gestured randomly. "She likes donuts, too."

"Maybe you can watch these two extra sacks for them, then," Maggie said. She handed over two more bags to the woman and looked over to where an older woman was sitting alone with a notebook in her lap.

She twirled a pen in her hand, and even from far away, Maggie could see her furrowed brows.

"Would you like a seat?" the woman asked. "You look like you've been working hard."

Maggie sighed. She looked around at the campsite. "You know, I would love to get off of my feet for a few minutes," she said. "I can't stay too long."

"I will take a few minutes of adult conversation," the woman said. She sat down at the picnic table next to her daughter and motioned for Maggie to take a seat across from her. "My husband and I run a small lure business. We spend a good part of the summer and the fall traveling to tournaments with the kids."

"You would never know you have ten kids by looking at this site or at you," she said. "How do you keep everything together so well?"

The woman shrugged. "Practice. Years and years of practice. I was a teacher before I quit and started having kids of my own. We never thought we would have ten!" She looked around and spoke quietly. "At first, we weren't sure we could have even one. And then, boom! Three sets of twins and one set of triplets."

"Oh, my goodness," Maggie said. "I can't even imagine!"

The woman shook her head and laughed. "Neither

could I, at first," she said. "Lacey here is the last little one and my only single birth. I'm Karen, by the way."

"I'm Maggie. And that's incredible. Do you homeschool, too?"

"I do, in fact. And the older kids help out with the business. We are very busy," Karen said. "But we travel together and camp together. Although, I think the next trip we are going to make is in an RV of our own. When my husband and the boys get back to camp this afternoon, I plan to inform him that we are going to retire the tents. Especially if my mother-in-law plans on joining us from now on. She assures us she just wanted to come along on this particular trip, but I'm not so sure why she chose this place of all the options. We travel quite a bit, and to some pretty nice places. Not that this place isn't nice…"

Maggie nodded her head. It seemed this woman did need some adult conversation, after all. "I can only imagine how hectic things can get for you. Dogwood Mountain is a beautiful town, but not exactly a tourist destination." She couldn't help but wonder, too, why Karen's mother-in-law had chosen this particular trip either. Of course, that's what happened when she started to become suspicious of everyone around her. "Where are you from?"

"Oh, we live outside Oklahoma City," Karen said.

"You probably think we're nuts for driving this far and sleeping in tents."

Maggie shook her head. "Oh, no, I don't think that," she said. "In fact. I met an older gentleman who said he was from somewhere northwest of Tulsa."

"You mean that writer who was killed?" Karen whispered. "What a shame that was."

Maggie nodded her reply.

"Anyway, I usually stay way out here and don't venture too far out near the lake when the tournament is going on, but I decided to talk a walk around to admire some of the big RVs a couple days ago." She laughed. "Like I said, I'm really over these tents, so I was checking out my options."

"I've met a few people around the lake that are quite interesting," Maggie said. "Although I can't say that I am in the market for an RV."

"Are you talking about buying an RV again?" Karen's mother-in-law came out of nowhere. "I'm Suze. And you are?"

"Maggie. It's nice to meet you." She gave the woman a once over. She wore a bucket hat, a torn flannel shirt, jeans with a thin, frayed rope as her belt, and no shoes on her feet. Something told her not to get on the lady's bad side. She looked to be about twenty years older than Maggie, but like she could also singlehandedly kick her butt with one hand tied behind her back.

"Mmhmm," the woman grunted. "I already told you that I don't think it's wise you waste your money."

"Suze, this kind woman came here to deliver us donuts, not listen to our family issues."

Maggie, feeling uncomfortable, changed the subject. "We weren't talking about RVs. We were talking about all the different people we've met around here so far. Especially, that poor writer... what was his name again?" She feigned ignorance and hoped for the best.

"Edward something, I think," Karen answered. "It was really early before the kids got up and my husband was still at the camp. I thought I was alone and when I heard his voice, he startled me."

Suze scoffed quietly, but Maggie heard it clear as day. "I never met any Edward," she said. "The only people I know about who are a little off are that man and his lady friend who were hollering all night. When she finally took off, I couldn't praise her enough. What a hassle that guy was. I don't even think they were staying in the campground, but they were all the way out here causing trouble anyway. I almost went out to take care of them myself because if they woke up these kids, I swear…"

Maggie's eyes widened. She looked at Karen. No one had ever said they were talking about anyone who was off as Suze had said, but Maggie was interested in the rest of the story.

"What were they hollering about, if you don't mind my asking?"

Karen reached inside a sack of mini donuts and pulled two out. She leaned in and lowered her voice. "There was a big discussion about the man who was killed. A lot of people were discussing him. Anyway, this guy started going on and on about how the man was a writer who betrayed his readers and his characters. He kept shouting louder and louder and his wife or girlfriend, whoever she was, tried to tell him to be quiet."

"Then what happened?" Maggie asked, barely able to contain herself.

"Sorry, I think I hear the kids calling," Suze said, taking a sack of mini donuts with her.

Maggie watched her as she left. She didn't like her. Hadn't known her for more than three minutes but didn't like her one bit.

"I don't know exactly, but you'll have to forgive Suze. She's a writer of sorts and seems to get herself

in a huff every time someone mentions the guy."
Maggie tried hard not to react as Karen continued.
"They weren't camping all the way out here. I think
they must have been visiting someone or taking a
walk and joined in on a conversation or something. I
saw the woman run off and he went racing after her.
Then when I talked to my husband later on when he
came back from the lake, he told me that she took the
car and their pop-up camper with her. She left him
with a tent but that's about it," Karen said. "After that,
he got into arguments with a few more people,
including my husband and another older man."

"Out of curiosity, was the guy around thirty,
maybe a little older, with darker hair and a beard?"

Karen nodded. "A very thick beard and leather
sandals," she said. "Why? Do you know who he is?"

"Unfortunately. I think I do," Maggie said. "His
name is Jeffrey. and he created a bit of an issue
outside of my food truck this morning."

"Was he the one the cops took away? I don't get
to see much all the way out here, but I hear plenty. I
always get so thrilled when my husband comes back
from where all the excitement is. It's like a little soap
opera out there."

"Not the cops, one cop. Brett. He's the chief of
police and a friend of mine. He arrested him because

he demanded free donuts and coffee and started kicking the back of the truck when I refused," Maggie said.

"I bet it was the same guy," Karen said.

"I think his girlfriend's name is Emily."

Karen nodded her head. "Yes, it has to be the same person, then," she said. "I think her dad is pretty popular in the fishing game." She shrugged. "All I know is that I hope that guy stays in jail or wherever he is. I like the peace and quiet when I can get it." Just then, an alarm of arguing children sounded and Karen laughed. "And it's not very often I get it."

CHAPTER TEN

Maggie returned to the food truck with her new friend's words in her head. Jeffrey sounded more and more like trouble to her. She reached the food truck and met Myra at the back door.

"What smells so good?" she asked when she walked inside. The food truck was filled with a sweet and savory aroma.

"Have a seat," Myra ordered. Maggie set the crate by the door and settled into a chair. Myra placed a tray in front of her and pointed to the box. "Open that."

Maggie complied. She pulled the edges of the brown cardboard lunch box apart. As soon as the food came into her view, she was overwhelmed with more of the delicious aroma.

"What is this?" she asked. "It smells so good."

"Well, you'll recognize Ruby's famous apple slaw with sliced pecans and cranberries added to it, but the sandwich is a grilled chicken Caprese panini," Myra said. "This is what I have been wanting to show you. I bought a small panini maker and have been torturing Orson with different recipes."

Maggie picked up the sandwich and took a bite. She instantly closed her eyes. "Oh, my gosh, that is so good," she said. "It's simply perfect."

"Well, thank you." Myra blushed slightly. "I was worried it wouldn't taste as good since you were gone longer than I expected."

"I know, and I'm sorry. I'll tell you all about it but first, I want to know more about this." She looked down at the panini.

"The thing about this is that you have a gourmet sandwich that can be prepped and made to order. I think the addition of a handful of recipes that we rotate through the week and three of these panini makers would be more than enough to keep up with demand."

"You want to add this to the menu at the donut shop?" Maggie asked.

Myra sat in the seat across the small table from her and nodded her head. "Absolutely, yes," she said.

"When we added the crockpot soups in the dead of winter, it brought in a new crowd later in the day. Our donut sales increased substantially. I think the panini option would be a good addition to the boxed lunches. In fact, I want to talk to you about a little bit of rebranding with our marketing. The bass tournament got me thinking about pushing the boxed lunches to tourist groups and travelers as they come off of the highway as well as strengthening our message to local employers."

"Whoa, whoa." Maggie held up her hands. "You're talking very fast, and I am having a hard time catching up. I'm on board with the paninis and the purchase of three panini makers. Actually, let's make it four so we have one for the food truck, too."

"Don't you want to try the other options first?" Myra asked.

Maggie shook her head. "If they are anything like this one, I'm sold," she said. "Now, tell me a little more about the boxed lunches."

Myra took a deep breath and spoke at a more even pace. "I think we should market the boxed lunches more to the takeaway crowd, maybe even offer delivery services for orders over a certain amount," she said. "We really want to encourage folks to call ahead and order for their employees or church groups for gatherings, and so on. Tourist groups on the highway could make arrangements for bulk orders as well."

"That would definitely help with prep work," Maggie said. "How are you going to encourage call-ahead orders?"

Myra smiled. Maggie knew Myra was getting to the part that she excelled at. "We're going to encourage bulk orders by offering a discount after a particular number. I also have quotes for ads in trade magazines and newsletters," she said. "We'll do the same in travel journals and websites. I think this is a really solid business idea."

"I think you're right," Maggie said. "Why don't you put together a small business plan and we can sit down with Ruby and start looking at the ads."

"Really?" Myra asked. She stood up and clasped her hands in front of her chest. "I have everything already on my laptop. I will absolutely get everything organized and in writing by next weekend."

"Let's plan a get-together," Maggie said. She was interrupted by a knock on the window.

"That'll be Brett." Myra headed to the door to let him in. "You're just in time."

"You offered me free food," Brett said. He smiled

broadly at Maggie and took the seat Myra had just vacated. "You say free food. I'll show up."

Maggie shook her head and dug into her apple slaw. She took one bite and shook her head again. "Oh, you are so right about this," she said. "The cranberries and the pecans add so much flavor."

Myra busied herself at the counter. She plated the panini for Brett and turned to the refrigerator. "Oh, no. I forgot the apple slaw for your plate, Brett," she said.

"That's okay," he said and picked up the fork she had placed in front of him. Before Maggie could think, Brett stood up slightly and leaned over. He speared his fork into her apple slaw and shoved down a bite.

"Oh, my gosh. You're absolutely right. That is delicious."

"Gee, Brett. Help yourself to mine," Maggie said.

"Thank you. I will." He helped himself to another bite and sat back down in his seat.

"You always were a hungry little boy beneath your charms," Maggie said.

"Did you just admit that you find me charming?" Brett asked. He reached for another bite. Maggie blocked him with her own fork. Within seconds, they had fallen into sword play.

"Children!" Myra stood three feet from them with one hand on her hip. She held the panini plate aloft in the other. "I don't want to have to separate you."

Brett dropped his fork and lowered his head. "She started it," he muttered. Maggie stared at him in shock for a moment, and then the giggles hit her. She bent over the table and shook with laughter. "I don't think I've ever affected you this much."

"Not since you stumbled on the field our senior year," Maggie said between giggles.

"Oh, now did you have to go and bring that up?" Brett said. He threw his fork on the table with extra dramatic flair.

"Okay, what am I missing here?" Myra asked. "And you better try that panini while it is still hot." Brett obediently picked up the sandwich and took a bite. He responded with a series of groans and moans.

"I guess that means he approves," Maggie said. Brett nodded vigorously. "Since he is busy stuffing his face, I will tell you the story." It felt so good to have a distraction and to laugh so hard.

"Oh, please do," Myra said. She checked over her shoulder to ensure no customers were waiting outside.

"Okay, during our senior year Brett was the quarterback on the football team. We were the Dogwood Mountain Huskies. Well, the football team decided that they wanted to take a different tack to raise money for the booster club."

"Maggie, you really don't have to share this story," Brett said.

"You just hush up and eat your panini," Myra scolded. "Please, continue."

"So, the football team, being the conscientious, fine young men that they were, devised a plan to raise money by competing with the cheerleaders during halftime at the homecoming game. The object was to compete for applause. They would each do a cheer and the crowd would respond. The principal and the superintendent were supposed to be the judges.

"The girls thought that they had it in the bag. They got ready and waited for the boys to come out of the locker room. All of a sudden the crowd went wild. Seven members of the football team ran out on the field in cheerleading outfits and Brett was the leader. Brett starts mucking with the crowd and dropped one of his fake embellishments out of his shirt, only he didn't see it. What he did was trip over it and start a chain reaction. One after another the quarterback and the offensive line were taken out by his ummm, well, embellishment."

Myra wheezed from laughter. Maggie shook her head and pounded the table. Brett sat back and pouted. His mouth and his shirt showed signs of his feast. He shook his head. "I can't believe you shared that story with her." He turned and wagged his finger at Myra. "If Brooks Macklin gets wind of that story, young lady."

"You're going to do what, Brett?" Maggie chuckled. "Act like a boob?"

"Very funny," Brett said. "And to think I was going to let you in on a little bit of information about the guy I arrested here this morning."

"Oh, Jeffrey? Actually," Maggie said and leaned forward. "I just might have some information for you."

Brett's eyes widened. "You have some information? Of course, you do."

Maggie nodded. "I went for a walk around the campground to hand out the leftover mini donuts. I ran into a woman with ten children at her campsite."

"Ten kids?"

"That's beside the point," Maggie said. "Anyway, she told me about a conversation that happened last night. Apparently, there was a loud discussion about Edmund Windsor's death. Jeffrey started carrying on about how he had betrayed his readers or something along those lines. The woman with him even told him to knock it off. They got into a fight, and she packed up the car and left."

"Do you know her name?" Brett asked.

"Emily," she replied. "I looked at his social media profile and I think her last name is Henson."

Brett pulled the notebook out of his front shirt pocket and began writing. "Are you sure the woman is gone? I think I need to have a conversation with her."

"I'm not sure of anything. I only saw her once, and I don't know anything about her other than the fact that her dad is a fisherman. But according to what I heard; she's gone."

"I think I'll take a walk down to the campground myself after I'm done here. Is there anything else you want to tell me?" Brett asked.

"The woman I talked to, her name is Karen, and her mother-in-law is Suze. I think there might be something up with her, but…

"Let me guess, you heard something about her, too? You know, Maggie, you can't believe everything you hear."

"I think he meant to say thank you, Maggie. What about you, Myra, you think that's what he meant?"

Brett shook his head and reached over to steal

CHAPTER ELEVEN

Maggie took her time walking back from the campground after she had introduced Brett to the woman named Karen. She found out from him on the way over that Jeffrey remained in the county jail. He was charged with disorderly conduct, and the officers were taking their time processing him. He vaguely said that it was likely more charges would be coming but wouldn't tell her anything more than that. It wasn't surprising though. There was no doubt that Jeffrey was a troublemaker.

When she returned to the food truck, Maggie decided to close down for the day. She informed Myra and turned off the sign. Her sides still ached from laughing earlier at Brett's expense, but her heart ached as well. She'd lost a new friend and her first real attempt at running the food truck in a place somewhere other than at the donut shop itself wasn't going exactly as planned. She might have been selling out of product nearly every day, but she was also feeling like she was going out of her mind. She decided that she would drop by the bookstore on the way home and pick up a copy of anything Edmund Windsor had written. The book she'd ordered online was due to arrive soon, but the truth was, she really wanted to read one of his horror novels. It would be new for her, but maybe the escape into something worse than what she was actually experiencing in real life, would help calm her nerves. Or make them worse. It was hard to tell, but she was curious, nonetheless. One thing she knew was that she wanted something physical to hold onto while she tried to understand his death.

Maggie pulled in front of Larabee's Books and Things and sighed before she went inside. Several cars were already in the parking lot. Maggie wondered if the others were there for the same reasons she was. From the outside, she could see the crowd gathered inside around a book display. She pushed the door open and hoped it was a new James Patterson or Nora Roberts release.

"Are you here for the Edmund Windsor display?" a wiry-haired woman asked when she entered. Her pale skin was blotched with red as she spoke. "Because if you are, you should know that we have completely sold out of any Neighborhood Watchers titles." She turned back to the crowd gathered around the display. "Did you all hear that? No more Neighborhood Watchers books. You are all wasting your time and mine!"

"Do you have any other Edmund Windsor titles?" Maggie asked, wondering why the other woman was so angry. The woman turned around and stared harshly at her.

"I have an entire shelf of his Crystal Kingdom series. But no one wants that one," she said. "The minute word of his death hit the internet; everyone went crazy for the horror series."

"I never even knew who he was until I met him," Maggie admitted to her quietly. "Mystery is more my genre. I just, well, he made an impression on me when I met him. I just wanted to get something he had written." She took the hint that the bookstore worker didn't want to hear that she, too, had come in looking for one of Edmund's horror novels.

"Wait, so you met him, and you didn't know who he was? That about figures," the woman said.

"I'm sorry, what?" Maggie asked. "What do you mean 'that about figures?'"

"Look, I have owned this bookstore for eighteen years. Once in a while, some author comes through here and stares at the hills around town for a few days. Only, most of them have the courtesy to let the local bookstore know when they come into town."

"Are you mad because Edmund didn't let you know he was in town?"

"Yeah, I am. I'm Faylene Larabee. My name is known among literary circles. This isn't a little bookstore stuck in some strip mall," she continued. "I've had this same location for almost twenty years. Writers from all over the world have come here and held book signings."

"You know, I never knew that," Maggie said, hoping to talk the woman down. It sure sounded like she was awfully angry at Edmund and that didn't sit right with her. "I'm really only interested in the first of one of his other series. Can you show me where I could find a copy? Mass market or paperback, it doesn't matter to me."

"You really are just an average reader, aren't you?" Faylene regarded her with slightly less disdain than she had when she first came in, yet Maggie wasn't so sure she was complimenting her." Follow me."

Maggie walked past the front counter and

followed Faylene toward the back of the store. They walked past the Neighborhood Watchers display. Maggie heard several people in the crowd arguing over the last title of the last book in the series. She tried to ignore their words and focus on where the bookstore owner led her.

The sooner she could get her book purchase made and get out of there, the sooner she could get home and rid herself of the stress of her day.

"You said you like mystery?" Faylene asked her from several steps ahead. "Who do you read?"

"I'm a big fan of Melville and Tucker," Maggie said. "And I like Burke Preston alone, too."

"Okay, so I would guess you own the Archie Hale series?"

Maggie smiled. "Every last volume," she said. "At least among those that have published so far."

"Favorite title?"

"Oh, gosh, that's tough," Maggie said. She named several favorites, and finally settled on her top three while Faylene listened intently.

Suddenly, Faylene's smile faded. She looked past Maggie and frowned. "What's going on now?"

Maggie turned slightly. She was aware of movement directly behind her and a change in the conversation.

"We might have a problem."

"What do you mean?" Maggie asked. As soon as she spoke, she felt a hard tap on her shoulder.

"What are you doing back here?" a man behind her asked. Maggie turned to look in his face, pinched with anger. "Well? You better start talking."

Maggie felt the muscles in her neck and upper back tense up. She balled her fists and narrowed her eyes at the man. "I better start talking? What is that supposed to mean?"

He took a step back and folded his arms over his chest. "I said what I said. You better start talking."

Faylene stepped around Maggie and confronted the man. "I think you need to leave right now," she said through clenched teeth. "I don't fancy people who threaten my customers."

"I'm your customer, too! And if you have some secret copies of the Neighborhood Watchers books hiding back here for your favored customers, you better show them to the rest of us," he snapped. Maggie noted his size for the first time. He was clearly over six feet tall and easily weighed over three hundred pounds.

"Don't threaten me," Faylene said.

"Show me what you have in your hand," the man

roared. He reached for the book in Faylene's hands and gripped it tightly.

"Let go," Faylene screamed. "Let go and get out of this store immediately! You aren't welcome here any longer!"

With the book still firmly in his hands, he pushed hard and sent Faylene sprawling backward. She landed with a thud on the wooden floor.

He turned his attention to Maggie. "You better show me what you got, too!"

"I better show you what I got, too? Do you even read books? Because you sound like an ignorant troll with a brain made of river mud," she shouted. Her entire body tensed. She stood on her toes and screamed in his face. "You will not put your hands on me, and you owe this woman an apology!"

"Lady, you're about to get it," he said and stuck his index finger in her face.

Maggie grabbed his finger in her hand and twisted it as hard as she could. "No, you're about to get it! I'm sick of you people! Did you even know the man you are so obsessed with? He was an old man. Just an old man with a brilliant gift and now he is dead. He's gone. He didn't owe any of you a thing," she shouted.

"Yes, he did," someone behind the big man shouted. "He owed us the rest of the Neighborhood

Watchers books! He cheated us out of the ending we deserved."

"He owed you? Who in the heck are you to think that he owed you anything?" Maggie continued to scream at the crowd. "Look at yourselves! An old man is murdered and here you are in a bookstore arguing with an old lady about the books she has available. And then you come along and push her to the ground!" She released the man's finger and reached her hand down to help Faylene back up to her feet.

"This is how you revere a writer you admire?"

"You don't have any idea what you're talking about, lady," the big man said. He reached his large hand around and gripped her by the back of her head. His fingers dug deep into her hair. "Now, you better show me what the old woman took you back here to see."

Maggie shoved the book Faylene had given her in his face. "Here! This is what she showed me," she yelled. "A paperback copy of his most famous fantasy novel. Not the one you think she showed me. One of the books you hated him for writing. Oh, and when you decided that we were back there discussing some top secret copies of his books, we were really talking about mystery novels."

The man tightened his grip on her hair. Maggie let out a shrill scream. She couldn't help it. The pain was too much. The crowd opened up around him. A second later, Maggie heard the unmistakable man's voice.

"If you know what's best for you buddy, you will let her go." Maggie merely wept at the familiar sound. "I'm the chief of police in this town, and you are in a mess of trouble. Don't make it worse for yourself."

The man held on for a second and then released her. She stumbled forward and fell into a book shelf. Faylene rushed to her side. "I'm so sorry," she said. "I had no idea things would get this bad."

"I had a bad feeling about it." Elias Cavanaugh appeared behind the rest of the people. "I'm the one who called the police."

"Thank you so much, Elias," Maggie said. She reached for his hand and held it for a moment. "This is absolutely nuts."

Brett was busy with the man who attacked her. He handcuffed him roughly and handed him over to another deputy. "The rest of you need to disperse. Get on out of here and leave this bookstore before I call the sheriff and check on the number of vacancies he has in the county jail."

Slowly the crowd began to move toward the door.

Brooks appeared and took Elias aside for his statement. Maggie checked with Faylene one more time.

"Here," the older woman said. "This is yours for the taking."

"You don't have to give me a book," Maggie said. "I came in here to buy one from you."

"You can buy the next one," Faylene said. "This one is on the house, as they say."

"Only if you promise to come by the donut shop tomorrow. Breakfast will be on the house," she said with a smile. "My business partner Ruby will set you right up."

"It's a deal," Faylene said. "And please accept my apology for my grumpiness when you first arrived. I have had too many days of this. The other morning, the very day Edmund Windsor was killed, these clowns were in here carrying on the same way."

Maggie held up her hands. "No apology needed after seeing what you've been dealing with," she said. "I just can't believe the insanity around all of this."

She thanked Faylene once more for the book and headed out into the parking lot. Brett stood beside her car when she walked out. He said nothing but took one step forward and enveloped her in an all-consuming hug.

CHAPTER TWELVE

It was late when Maggie returned to the donut shop. After the events of the day, she decided to skip going home to read and instead head to the donut shop to handle the preparations that would make her life at the food truck easier the following morning. Over and over in her mind, she debated whether she should just close it down for the rest of the tournament.

The plan had been to remain open one day beyond the end of the tournament, but Maggie questioned the purpose now. What she really wanted to do was drive the truck back to the donut shop parking lot, return the keys to her office, and go home to bed for those final two days.

Her head still ached from the death grip the man in the bookstore had on her hair. Maggie wished she'd been able to seek the refuge of her comfortable bed with a good book and let the world continue without her for a little while, but reality and her overactive brain would not allow for that. So, she got busy doing the things she knew had to be done for the following day. She was alone at the donut shop, but before she finished mixing the first batch of cinnamon roll dough, she picked up her phone and texted Ruby.

"I'm at the shop doing prep for the morning," she wrote.

"I'll be there in ten minutes," Ruby replied.

"Oh, you don't have to come down here," Maggie said aloud in the empty kitchen. "Not necessary," she wrote back in a text.

"Don't care. Be there soon," Ruby replied again.

Maggie was quite glad that Ruby decided to come over. Being alone never really fazed her much, but after the incident at the bookstore, having her best friend around sounded like a good idea. She'd just likely never admit it out loud.

When Ruby arrived, Maggie had just put the second batch of cinnamon roll dough into the cooler to rest until she picked it up in the morning. She decided not to make another trip down to the lake that night. She would do what she had to do at the donut shop, and then turn around and go back home to bed.

"What can I do?" Ruby asked when she plucked her apron off of the hook outside of the storeroom.

"Pull up a stool and keep me company." Most of the work Ruby could do had been done. The boxed lunches were already prepared and in the cooler. Everything else would be made on-site in the food truck.

"What do you think of Myra's panini plan?" Ruby asked.

"I think I have never tasted such a delicious hot sandwich in all of my days." Maggie smiled. "Her plan sounds solid and well thought out. Did you know about any of this?"

Ruby shrugged. "I may have given her the funds to purchase the panini maker. But the rest of it was all her doing."

"I think we should go through the food truck once this lake tournament thing is behind us and make sure we have everything planned efficiently, especially with the addition of the paninis," Maggie said. "We'll have to adjust the menu board anyway."

"This trip hasn't panned out like we hoped it would," Ruby observed.

"Actually, in terms of sales, we've far exceeded what we thought we'd make out there," Maggie said.

"It's all of this other mess that's cast a shadow over the whole affair."

Ruby pulled a second stool out of the storeroom and set it a few feet from her own. "Let's have a seat and chat for a moment," she said.

"Have a seat? I don't have a lot of time right now," Maggie argued.

"Yes, you do," Ruby insisted. "Sit."

Maggie complied. She settled onto the stool and rested her elbows on the baker's table. "Alright, I did need that," she said and sighed.

"It's been a lot this week, hasn't it?"

Maggie nodded. "I made a friend, and then he was murdered. And I am so much sadder about that than it feels like I ought to be."

"Sometimes, people breeze in and out of our lives and make quite the impact on us, even if they were only there for a short time," Ruby said quietly. "I suspect Edmund Windsor was that way for you."

Maggie nodded. Tears stung her eyes, and she buried her head in her hands. "It seems so stupid to be so sad about this," she said. A second later, a torrent of tears flowed down her face. She was aware of Ruby's arms around her shoulders as she cried.

"Oh, my gosh," she said when her sobs were

finished. "I don't do that. I don't cry. I'm not a crying person. I don't know where that came from."

Ruby released her hug and returned to her stool. "It came from grief. I've been accused of being too stoic in my life, Maggie. But the day I walked back out to my car from the funeral home when my father died," Ruby said and shook her head at the memory. "It took three people from the funeral home to help me back inside. I was overcome by grief. But then, it was over, and I felt better able to deal with his loss."

"You never shared that with me," Maggie said. "I'm so sorry about your dad."

"It's just not something I talk about. Sort of like feelings in general for you," Ruby smiled. "Brett told me what happened at the bookstore. You've been through a lot over the past few days."

"I'll survive," Maggie said.

"Of course, you will, but there is more to life than mere survival."

Maggie stood up and stretched her arms over her head. Her back ached more than normal. "I just can't understand why Edmund was murdered," she said. "It's so hard to believe that one of his fans would have been angry enough with him for not finishing a series to kill him over it."

"Is that the only option?" Ruby asked. "I mean, do you think there may be another motive?"

Maggie was about to tell her about Faylene and how upset she seemed about Edmund not telling her that he was in town, when the door handle on the back door turned. Orson and Myra walked in, followed by Brooks and Brett. "We heard that there was a party here," Myra announced. She carried a stack of boxes in her arms.

"What is that?" Ruby asked.

"This?" Brooks asked. He sported three boxes himself. "This is a family-size order of brick-oven baked authentic Italian pizzas."

"You guys are crazy," Maggie said. "Let's go out front."

Myra bolted ahead of her and set the pizza boxes in a line on the front counter. Brooks followed suit. Brett and Orson moved the tables and chairs around so they could all eat seated around one large table, family-style.

They passed around the pizza and chatted easily for a while. Maggie felt her spirits rise with each moment that passed. Only once did she break her attention away from the rest of the table to check a text on her phone. When she opened the text she smiled. Bradley had sent her a photo of Wyatt smiling for the first time.

"Ruby," she said and passed the phone around to her. For the next few moments, the comments around the table were directed to her and her adorable grandson.

"You look pensive," Brett said when he handed her phone back. "Are you missing the boys?" Since their stay in Dogwood Mountain, Bradley, and little Wyatt had come to be known as "the boys" among her friends.

"Always," Maggie admitted. "I was just thinking about something Edmund said to me. He spoke about taking the time to immerse himself in things. In his case, it was the worlds he wrote about. That's why a number of his fans were so disgruntled with him. He started a series that he said he couldn't get into, so he ended it halfway through where he had planned to go."

"That's interesting," Brooks said and cast a look at Brett.

"But that's not what was on my mind," Maggie said. "I was just thinking about his comments. Do you know? Living life so authentically. He was a simple man. He loved to take walks along the lake because he couldn't enjoy actually going in the water himself."

"Wait, why couldn't he enjoy the water?" Brett asked.

"I don't know, some sort of allergy or something," Maggie said. "One morning he was caught out in the rain and his skin broke out in red splotches."

"Like hives?" Brooks asked.

"Exactly like hives," Maggie replied. "Why do I think your questions have more to do with the death investigation than my reminiscences?"

"I'm sorry, Maggie," Brett said. "But you might have just given us some information that will help this case. We've been beating our heads against the wall, trying to figure out where to go from here."

"I don't understand," Myra spoke up. "What does the water have to do with the old man's death?"

"Watch who you're calling an old man," Orson muttered next to her.

"I was referring to the author who died," Myra said back to him.

"Yeah, well Edmund Windsor wasn't that much older than me," Orson said.

"Anyway, when Mr. Windsor was found, his clothes were wet and we assumed that he might have gone wading on the shore and fallen into the lake," Brett explained.

"But he wasn't found anywhere near the shore, was he?" Maggie said.

"Exactly right," Brett continued. "Not like we thought at first. His skin was red and raw under where his clothes were still damp. Brooks here suggested a water allergy, but the medical examiner dismissed that outright."

"He said a water allergy is extremely rare," Brooks said. "But it only makes sense because his skin was normal everywhere else."

"He told me flat out that he couldn't enjoy the water," Maggie said. "Even rain."

"Sounds like *aquagenic urticaria*," Brooks said.

"Come again," Ruby said.

"That's the official name of this rare water allergy," Brett said. "I need to make a quick phone call." He got up from the table and stepped inside the kitchen.

"He'll be calling the coroner," Brooks said. "I think you may have just helped crack this case wide open, Maggie."

CHAPTER THIRTEEN

Maggie headed out to the lake for the last time the following morning. She discussed the decision with Ruby before they left the donut shop the night before. Given everything that had happened, there was nothing to be gained by leaving the food truck for an extra day.

"We made out like bandits on the days you were there," Ruby had told her. "You should take off an extra day. Stay home and rest."

Maggie dismissed the idea initially, but as the day wore on she considered it more and more.

Just after seven, Maggie looked out at the crowd gathered to purchase their coffee and donuts from her. She waved when she saw Karen and was thankful Suze didn't appear to be in sight.

"Did you get away for some sanity this morning?" Maggie asked.

"Something like that," Karen said. "We are leaving this afternoon and I wanted to make sure we patronized your business at least once while we're still around. I thought having my mother-in-law along on this trip to help me with the kids would have been nice, but this is one of two times that she's offered to help out, so I took advantage and decided to come here. She certainly doesn't mind asking me for help, though…" She sighed and placed her large order then.

"I appreciate your business, but you're under no obligation to make such a large order," Maggie said.

"Oh, yes I am," Karen said and laughed. "My husband and the older kids got back and loved those donuts so much, he wanted me to come straight down here and pick some up for a treat after dinner. I told him the food truck closed after lunch, so he woke up early and reminded me to head down here this morning."

"Did everything remain quiet yesterday?"

Karen nodded. "To be honest, I haven't seen half of the people that were hanging around before," she said.

Maggie bagged up her order and handed it over.

She thought of the incident at the bookstore. "Have you heard anything more about that author?"

Karen laughed. "It's been radio silence on the writer since yesterday. I am beginning to wonder if Jeffrey wasn't the biggest problem with all of that." She thanked Maggie for the donuts and left.

Maggie thought about her words for the rest of the morning. A few minutes before noon, Brett and Brooks appeared at the order window.

"I sure hope you have some cinnamon rolls left," Brett said. Maggie smiled and produced two extra-large cinnamon rolls from the refrigerator.

"Any news on Edmund's death?" she asked timidly.

Brett cast a wary look at Brooks. "It's hit a bit of a roadblock," he said.

"Meaning what, exactly?" Maggie asked.

Brett sighed deeply. Brooks took over and explained, "We had to release Jeffrey."

"What? Why? I thought he was your prime suspect!"

"We didn't have anything to hold him on," Brett said.

"There wasn't enough to charge him with Edmund's death, Maggie. In fact, Jeffrey was seen in the bookstore causing a fuss around the time the coroner put the approximate time of death," Brooks said.

"He couldn't have been the one, then," Maggie said. She turned to Brett. "Have you made another arrest? You were there yesterday at the bookstore. There are at least a dozen other people who could have harmed Edmund."

"And we are checking on each of them," Brett said. "That's how we know Jeffrey was there and not at the lake."

Maggie sighed and nodded. Brett had never left any stone unturned in an investigation she was privy to, not once. It wasn't that she didn't trust him. Not at all.

After Brooks and Brett walked back up the trail to the parking lot, Maggie glanced at the clock. It was a few minutes past noon, and she decided it was quitting time. Whatever she would gain by staying there a few more hours wasn't worth it. In short order she had the machines shut down and the small kitchen cleaned up. The next step was a brief phone call to Orson at the donut shop.

"I didn't expect for you to call so soon," he said.

"Neither did I," Maggie said. "But I am finished. I am ready to be out of here."

"Why don't you come on back here and I'll ride back over with you to drive the truck back," he said.

Maggie smiled and hung up the phone. It felt good to lock up the door and head to her car. It felt like action after days of stagnation. She was finished with the bass tournament and the bad memories that came with it.

As she walked toward her car, she heard someone call out to her. "Oh, hey there," the voice said. Maggie turned to see the man from the bookstore waving at her. Elias Cavanaugh walked toward her. His face had become familiar around the lake as well. "Are you shutting down?"

Maggie stopped just outside her car. "I am," she said. "I think I've done all of the damage I can do. And the atmosphere just isn't the same now."

"Yeah, I can see how this week's events would put a damper on everything," he said.

Maggie unlocked her door and rested her arm on the roof. "So, how did you do?"

"How did I do?"

"In the tournament," Maggie asked. "How were the fish biting?"

Elias glanced toward the lake. "Oh, well, I didn't have much luck," he said. "I spent a lot of the time in my fifth wheel camper reading."

"Oh, well," Maggie said. "I hope you have a safe

trip back home." She waved at the man and turned to get in her car. He stood watching her for a moment and then walked back toward where the RVs were parked.

Orson stood just outside of the donut shop when she pulled into the parking lot a few minutes later to pick him up. He smiled when he opened her car door and stepped in.

"Are you sure that you don't want to drive the truck back yourself? I can certainly follow behind in your car," he said.

"If you don't mind, I would rather not stretch my comfort zone that much," Maggie said. She pulled to a stop as close to the trail as she could. "Are you up for the walk down that way?" she asked.

"You forget how much I walk around town, my dear," Orson said. He opened the car door and stood up. "The campground empties almost as quickly as it fills up. But I see a few more people out on the lake."

Maggie laughed. "I don't think they're ready to give it up just yet," she said. "Well, some of them. I swear I actually met a few people that seemed more interested in Edmund Windsor than the bass tournament."

Orson narrowed his eyes slightly. "I heard about what happened at the bookstore," he said.

"That was a terrible experience," Maggie said. "But even here. I met people here that seemed uninterested in bass fishing."

Orson's eyes narrowed slightly. Maggie braced herself for one of his scathing one-liners. Instead, he shot her a sideways look. "You met people here in the campground who were more interested in a reclusive writer than the fishing tournament?"

Maggie nodded. "I guess you could say I met quite a few strange folks this week," she said. "Oh, well. Are you ready to roll?"

Orson nodded and headed toward the food truck. A few minutes later, he had the truck headed slowly out of the RV space and back up toward the road. She turned her car around and followed behind him. They drove slowly around the lake and toward the road to town. Orson drove cautiously toward the stop sign but stopped the truck. Maggie watched as the reverse lights flashed momentarily.

"What's going on, Orson? Why did you put it in park?" She waited for him to climb out of the truck and walk back to her car to let her know what was going on, but he never left the truck. Instead, he hit the brakes and put the truck back in drive. He waited for a lumbering camper to pass and finally went on his way.

Despite his caution around the lake, Orson drove quickly back to the donut shop. Maggie thought about calling him but decided to wait until they got back. Not knowing what might be wrong made her less inclined to add any sort of distraction while he drove.

"What's the matter," she asked him as soon as they arrived at the donut shop. "You waited for a while at the stop sign and then drove pretty intensely all the way back."

"I didn't drive in any way that should raise any alarms for you," Orson snapped. "As you can see, the truck is here and in one piece."

"Orson, you know that's not what I was implying," Maggie said. "I want to know what's going on with you."

Orson folded his arms and leaned against the truck. "Gretchen LeClair called me on the way over. That's when I pulled to a stop. She said something is going on at the Dogwood House," he said.

"Something odd. She's hearing noises in Edmund's room."

"He still has a room there?"

Orson nodded. "She said he was paid up through the end of the month. She's hesitant to disturb anything. The police have already been there of course, but she is waiting for his brother to come and claim his belongings."

"But she's hearing things? Like what?"

"Typing, papers shuffling," he said. "She wouldn't admit it, but I think she's concerned that the room is haunted or something."

"Why don't you head over there and keep her company for a while?" Maggie said. "I'm sure she would like a friend around."

"I think I will," Orson said. He turned to her and smiled slightly. "Maybe an old man like me can still provide a lady a sense of protection."

Maggie patted his arm and walked beside him back to the donut shop.

CHAPTER FOURTEEN

Maggie unpacked the food truck quickly and went in one last time. She had no plans for the truck to be used for a little while and wanted to make sure it was thoroughly cleaned out.

"You need to go on home and have a hot bath or something," Ruby told her when she came back inside the shop. "I can see the tension all over your face."

"It's been a rough week, that's for sure," Maggie said. She set the last of the trays down at the sink. "I'll get these cleaned up and get out of here."

"No, we've got it," Myra said. "It's slow right now. Orson is still at the Dogwood House. I'll get these trays washed up and put away. You take care of yourself for a little while."

Maggie took their advice to heart and drove the

short distance to her small cottage home. She thought of her Aunt Marjorie as she walked through the back door and wondered if life at the donut shop was ever quite as eventful.

After a hot shower, Maggie brewed a cup of tea and settled into her overstuffed chair in the living room. An alert on her phone reminded her that Edmund's book would be arriving soon. She picked up the volume she had been given by Faylene at the bookstore and thumbed through the first pages. Finding it too hard to concentrate, she closed the book again. Her mind wandered to the bookstore. One of the angry faces might have been the person who killed her friend.

Maybe it was the man who grabbed her by the arm and shoved the bookstore owner to the floor. She glanced at her phone, tempted to call Brett, and grill him over the status of the investigation. But surely, she thought, Brett had considered the man he had arrested for the skirmish. Maybe it was Suze, who seemed to just be an overall odd character. Karen had said she was a writer and maybe as a fellow writer she was angry with Edmund for not finishing his series for his readers. On the other hand, Maggie knew Edmund was a private person and if his death had something to do with his water allergy, it was likely that whoever killed him, had known that tidbit about him.

She set the book to the side and padded across the room to her bedroom. She picked up her laptop and returned to her seat. Brett didn't need her questions about the investigation, but Maggie needed to feel like she was helping out in some way. She opened her laptop and googled the bass tournament. Maybe there were pictures already posted to social media. Maybe she could find a few faces and compare them to the crowd at the bookstore.

She searched the name of the tournament and scrolled through a few social media profiles with recent photos tagged with the event. But most of the photos were taken of one or two people at the same time on a boat in the middle of the lake. Other photos focused on the lake or their prize-winning catches, and not people.

Frustrated, Maggie decided to search for the name of the lake instead. She typed "Dogwood Mountain Lake" and waited. A few seconds later, Maggie scrolled through several more photos, some more than a year old. She scanned a few pages and stopped at a new hashtag. "Edmund Windsor sighting Dogwood Mountain, Missouri." She hastily clicked on the hashtag. Her screen was populated with hundreds of photo results. Most of the pictures were taken over the past few days. She scrolled through and held her breath. A number of the photos included dark, grainy pictures of Edmund walking along the lake.

The majority of the photos were taken early in the morning. She found a few of herself seated on the park bench watching the waves roll in during the moments before dawn. The captions echoed the hostile words she had heard from the mob in the bookstore.

Maggie continued to read. Her heart beat harder in her chest the further she read.

"Make him finish, hashtag Neighborhood Watchers!"

"Find Edmund Windsor!"

"Make him write!"

Maggie copied the photos and the captions and attached them to an email. She sent the email to Brett at the police department and then opened her phone to text him. "See email. I'm not sure if you have seen these or not," she wrote.

Maggie set her phone down and hurried back through the pictures' hashtags. She found another interesting tag at the end of nearly every hashtag thread. "Defender of the Neighborhood Watchers." She quickly opened a new web search for the hashtag.

Immediately she found a website dedicated to Edmund Windsor's defunct book series and several recent photographs from the lake.

The website was filled with more rantings like she heard at the bookstore. She found dozens more photos of Edmund taken in different places. The dates on the photos went back many months, even years. There were pages filled with information about his writing habits, his various home addresses, and even his rare allergy to fresh water.

"Oh, you poor man," Maggie said. "They hunted and stalked you for years."

She flipped through more pages. There were rants made into memes, even a few animated posts that depicted Edmund as a prisoner in a cell writing feverishly under force. Maggie shook her head and shut the computer lid. Maggie texted Brett and told him what she found and to check his email. Right away he replied back and told her to see if she recognized any familiar faces in the photos on the website. Maggie didn't bother to reply. She opened her laptop lid once more. She scoured the photos as fast as she could. Tension built in her mind as she looked.

Maybe Brett was on to something.

Maggie jumped between the website and the social media photos. After a few minutes, she started to lose hope. She saw several faces, but none struck a familiar chord with her.

Until she returned to the website and decided to check out the page titled "about me." She scrolled through another rambling diatribe about Edmund and his abandonment of the Neighborhood Watchers series. Maggie scrolled through the many paragraphs until she reached the bottom of the screen. At the bottom of the webpage was a tiny thumbnail photo of the self-described webmaster with the moniker "Neighborhood Watchers Defender." Maggie clicked on the photo to blow it up.

Immediately, she knew who he was. She pulled her phone off of the arm of the chair and typed out a text to Brett. She moved her fingers as fast as she could. "Elias Cavanaugh," Maggie wrote. "The webmaster is Elias Cavanaugh."

"Where can I find him?" Brett texted back right away.

Maggie thought for a moment. Frustrated with texting back, Maggie hit the phone icon on her screen and waited for him to answer. "What's up?" he asked when he answered.

"Elias said he was in a fifth-wheel camper." She thought back to the first day she'd met him and remembered not only that, but that he'd said he was good with computers and liked photography. Jeffrey was a jerk, but it was Elias who was the real problem.

"Elias Cavanaugh is a fake name," Brett told her. "We already found him. His real name is Alfred Greeley and he's listed as a guest at the Dogwood House."

Maggie felt her stomach drop to the floor. "Brett, Orson went over there because Gretchen was worried about noises she heard coming from Edmund's room," she said. "You have to get over there."

CHAPTER FIFTEEN

The following night, Maggie tucked her legs under her and gazed at the popping flames in the bonfire. She rested her hand on the glass on the arm of the chair beside her. Ruby had made it plainly obvious that she was there to relax. It was her day off and she was surrounded by her friends.

She glanced over at Orson, who sat taller in his Adirondack chair than she had ever seen. Gretchen LeClair was seated to his right. Her chair was quite close to his. Maggie smiled. For once, the older gentleman was a hero to someone.

"The sheriff took Greeley off of our hands almost as soon as he was arrested," Brooks said.

"I still think of him as Elias Cavanaugh," Maggie admitted.

"He's a very bad dude, no matter what his name is," Brooks said.

"But, he is behind bars now," Gretchen added. She beamed at Orson. "It sends shivers down my spine to think that he was in Edmund's room."

"But at least you know it wasn't a ghost," Myra said with a laugh.

Brett spoke up at last. "What I don't understand is how a group of people could have such an intense devotion to a book series," he said. "So much so that they would follow an old man and try to force him to finish the last book the way they wanted him to write it."

"Is that what happened?" Ruby asked. "This Cavanaugh character tried to force Edmund Windsor to rewrite the novel?"

"Elias said he went fishing later in the day, but I don't think he went at all. I think he found out about Edmund being in town and came under the guise of being there for the tournament. Same with Jeffrey. Either that or it was pure luck that he was here anyway to try to impress his girlfriend's dad. Not that I think he did a very good job at that." Maggie chuckled.

"I agree," Brett said. "When we got to Dogwood House, we found him in Windsor's room. We think he tried to force Windsor to rewrite the series and when that didn't go as planned, he may have tried stealing his notes to see if he could end the series himself."

"So he'd get the credit?" Myra asked.

"That's what we're thinking," Brett said.

"So, what happened the day he was killed?" Ruby asked. She set another tray of grilled flatbread on the table in the center of the circle of chairs. "And just to be sure, Greeley and Cavanaugh are the same person, right?"

"Right," Brett replied. "Greeley is Cavanaugh's real name."

"Well, surprise of all surprises, the bad guy isn't talking," Brooks said. "But from what we have put together, he checked into the Dogwood House under a false name, just so he wouldn't tip Windsor off to who he was."

"The poor old man had been badgered by these folks for so many years it's likely that he had come across him before," Brett said. "The bass tournament was a good guise for Greeley to be here." He smiled at Maggie.

"And he called the cops that day at the bookstore just to look good, then," Maggie said.

Brett nodded. "That's what we believe. He must have confronted Windsor in his room that day. He somehow forced him to go to the lakeshore and threatened him," he said. "We had evidence that he forced him into the water."

"That explains why his clothes were wet and his skin was so bad," Maggie said. "Greeley used his allergy to torture him into compliance."

Brooks and Brett both nodded. "And when that didn't work, Greeley strangled him."

"Just think, if he had come after me, you would have been there to defend me," Gretchen said. She beamed at Orson again.

Orson merely blushed and sat up higher in his chair.

Maggie listened as the discussion continued. She sipped her drink and watched the flames crackle in the bonfire. She gazed upward and wondered about the old man and his legacy. Would anyone collect his writings and secure them from the masses? Now that he was dead, would the cult-like followers finally let him rest? She hoped Greely hadn't gotten too much information and would stay in prison long enough to never be able to put out any of Edmund's ideas, if he had.

"Something on your mind?" Brett leaned in and asked her quietly.

Maggie shook her head. "Just thinking about

Edmund. He was such a kind man, and so smart. I just don't know why those people couldn't have left him alone," she said. "His life was unfairly daunted by the stress and anxiety those people caused him."

"And yet, he still found time for early morning walks and a love for sitting in nature, just taking it in. Isn't that what you told me before?" Brett said.

Maggie nodded. "Still, what a waste of his time. How unfair that he had to live under that constant threat, all because he wrote a book but didn't finish things the way others wanted."

Maybe," Brett said, and gently laid his hand on top of hers. "Maybe his ability to take walks and watch the waves roll in was the best revenge. They tried to rob him of his peace to force him to give them what they wanted, but he had it in here all along." Brett gently tapped the front of his shirt.

Maggie felt the warmth of his hand on her own. She stared into the fire and wondered about all of the things she would miss about her life if she was forced away from the peace she had come to find among her friends.

***

If you enjoyed Knead 'Em and Weep, check out the next book in the series, Fried and True, today!

AUTHOR'S NOTE

I'd love to hear your thoughts on my books, the story-lines, and anything else that you'd like to comment on —reader feedback is very important to me. My contact information, along with some other helpful links, is listed on the next page. If you'd like to be on my list of "folks to contact" with updates, release and sales notifications, etc.… just shoot me an email and let me know. Thanks for reading!

Also…

… if you're looking for more great reads, Summer Prescott Books publishes several popular series by outstanding Cozy Mystery authors.

CONTACT SUMMER PRESCOTT
BOOKS PUBLISHING

Blog and Book Catalog: http://summerprescottbooks.com

Email: summer.prescott.cozies@gmail.com

And…be sure to check out the Summer Prescott Cozy Mysteries fan page and Summer Prescott Books Publishing Page on Facebook – let's be friends!

To sign up for our fun and exciting newsletter, which will give you opportunities to win prizes and swag, enter contests, and be the first to know about New Releases, click here: http://summerprescottbooks.com

Made in United States
North Haven, CT
15 March 2023